Tumblebugs and Hairy Bears

Exploring Insects With Children

by Suzanne Samson

illustrations by Preston Neel

ROBERTS RINEHART PUBLISHERS

Boulder, Colorado

For Grandma,
and thanks dad, for sharing your interest in insects with me.
Suzanne M. Samson

For Maggie, my loving wife.
Preston Neel

Text Copyright © 1996 by Suzanne Samson
Illustrations Copyright © 1996 by Preston Neel
International Standard Book Number 1-57098-088-8
Library of Congress Catalog Card Number 96-67080

Published by
Roberts Rinehart Publishers
5455 Spine Road, Boulder, Colorado 80301

Published in the U.K. and Ireland by
Roberts Rinehart Publishers
Trinity House, Charleston Road
Dublin 6, Ireland

Distributed in the U.S. and Canada by Publishers Group West

Printed in Canada

Flying, crawling or hanging around,
Incredible insects might be found.
So be alert throughout the day,
You might just find, along your way...

Lovebugs kissing their spouses, or...

Carpenter Ants building houses, or...

Bed Bugs being shown the door, or...

Dance Flies soaring across the floor, or...

Mining Bees searching for gold, or...

Walkingsticks supporting the old, or...

Clown Beetles amusing crowds, or...

Rain Beetles dancing under clouds, or...

A Fishfly catching a trout, or...

Tent Caterpillars camping out, or...

Stink Bugs behaving quite rude, or...

Harvester Ants gathering food, or...

Ambush Bugs surprising a bee, or...

Gypsy Moths dancing festively, or...

Fire Ants extinguishing flames; or...

Goldsmith Beetles engraving names, or...

Water Boatmen out to sea, or...

Vampire Leafhoppers in a tree, or...

A Green Darner mending clothes, or...

Painted Ladies striking a pose, or...

Potter Wasps throwing some clay, or...

Great Purple Hairstreaks turning grey, or...

Tumblebugs rolling here and there, or...

Acrobatic Ants flying through the air, or...

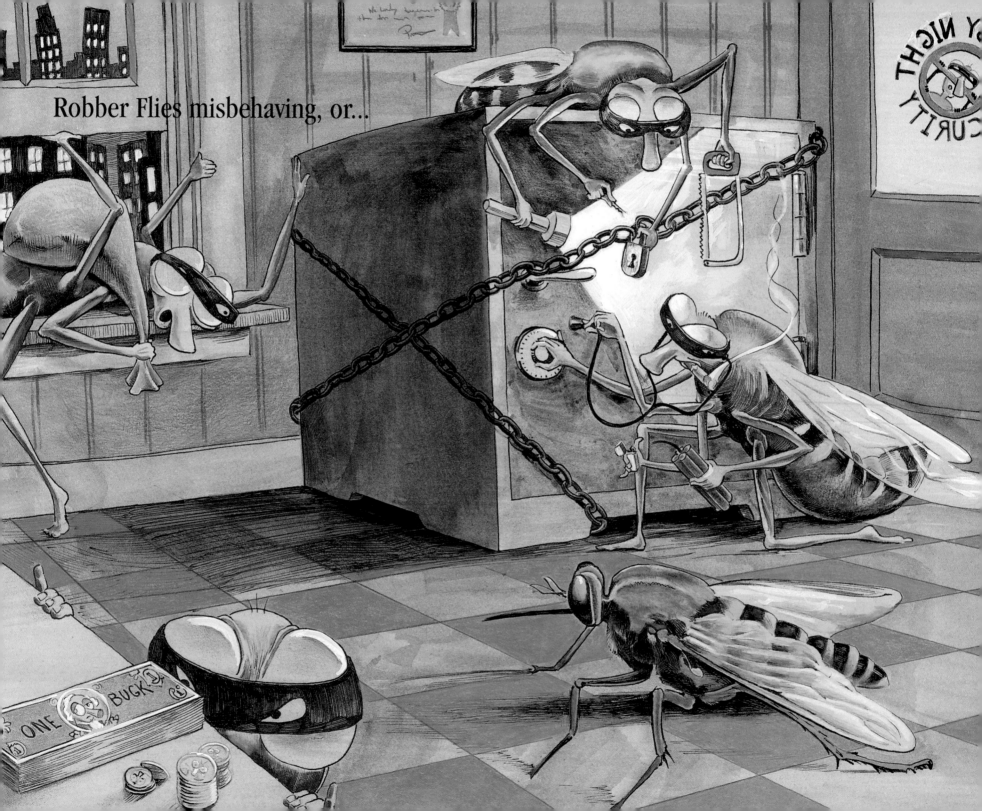

Robber Flies misbehaving, or...

Hairy-legged flies busily shaving, or...

WHAT ATLAS SAID TO HERCULES

BEE FIT

Sweat bees working out in a gym, or...

Hairy Bear Beetles receiving a trim.

Please, appreciate each sight.
But don't dare touch – avoid a bite!

REFERENCES

Simon & Schuster's Guide to Insects, by Ross H. Arnett, Jr., Ph.D. and Richard L. Jacques, Jr., Ph.D.

The Audubon Society Field Guide to North American Insects & Spiders, by Lorus and Margery Milne

GLOSSARY

Lovebug
Plecia neartica
Grows to about 14 mm.
Low vegetation, grasslands.
Southeast U.S., westward to Texas.

Carpenter Ant
Camponotus ferrugineus
Grows up to 13 mm.
Wood nesters, grasslands.
Eastern U.S. and Canada, westward to Texas.

Bed Bug
Cimex lectularius
Grows to 7 mm.
Found in houses, especially bedrooms.
Global.

Dance Fly
Empis spp.
Grows to 5 mm.
Found on flowers and plants in gardens, fields and meadows.
United States.

Willow Mining Bee
Andrena salicifloris
Grows to 14 mm.
Found in the mountains and arid regions.
California to Colorado and as far north as British Columbia.

Northern Walkingstick
Diapheromera femorata
Can grow to 95 mm.
Found in trees and shrubs in deciduous forests.
Eastern U.S. and Canada, westward to New Mexico.

Flat Clown Beetle
Hololepta populnea
Grows to about 9 mm.
Woods, commonly found on willow and poplar trees.
Throughout the Rocky Mountain region of the U.S.

Rain Beetle
Pleocoma hirticollis
Grows to about 25 mm.
Forest.
California.

Fishfly
Chauliodes spp.
Found among plants along streams.
Throughout the U.S., Canada and Mexico; more restricted areas for individual species.

Tent Caterpillars
Malacosoma species
Adult wingspan to 38 mm.
In woods; also in cultivated trees such as apple and wild cherry.
Various species throughout the U.S., Canada and Mexico.

Two-spotted Stink Bug
aka Conspicuous Stink Bug
Cosmopepla conspicillaris
About 7 mm.
Found in open areas such as fields and meadows.
Eastern North America (east of the Rocky Mountains).

Rough Harvester Ant
Pogonomyrmex rugosus
Grows to about 7 mm.
Sandy areas.
Southwestern U.S.; also found in Mexico.

Jagged Ambush Bug
Phymata erosa
About 10 mm.
Camouflage themselves among flowers in gardens and meadows.
United States and southern parts of Canada.

Gypsy Moth
Lymantria dispar
Male wingspan is about 20 mm., female wingspan up 70 mm.
Forests.
Primarily found in the northestern regions of the U.S. and along the southern border of Canada.

Fire Ant
Solenopsis geminata
Workers grow up to 6 mm.
Can be found in open fields or woods.
Found in the Gulf states to the Pacific Coast and as far north as British Columbia.